ROAD CLOSED

ROAD CLOSED

JAN MARK

*Hodder
Children's
Books*

A division of Hodder Headline Limited

For Louis Attlee

1

When Connie arrived at Gran's on Thursday night, the signs were already in the front garden, leaning against the bird bath. On Friday someone delivered four sandbags, the kind that people use to keep water out of their houses when rivers flood, but Gran lived a long way from the river.

At 9.40 on Saturday morning Abdul and Ahmed from next door came round with a barrow that had four uprights in it, almost as tall as Connie. They loaded up the signs and the sandbags and at 9.50 they all set out, down to the end of the street where it met the main road.

The signs read, ROAD CLOSED. They were like the ones you saw when the water company or the gas and electricity people were going to dig up the street. Connie felt important, helping to put up signs like that, although no one was going to dig up Lancaster Street. Ahmed was carrying the crossbars by himself, one over each shoulder. He was still at school but he was very tall and had a moustache. He walked in front, balancing along the kerb stones like someone on a tightrope.

All the time they were pushing the barrow down Lancaster Street no cars passed them, but as soon as they reached the junction a post office van turned the corner, then a pick-up truck, heading for the garage in Brookes Road. Lancaster Street was one-way. Drivers used it as a short cut but now they had only three more minutes to do it in, until ten o'clock tomorrow morning.

Ahmed and Abdul stood on one side of the street, Gran and Connie on the other.

Gran was looking at her watch. When there was only half a minute to go she started a countdown. '29, 28, 27, 26 . . .'

Two cars came round the corner.

'15, 14, 13, 12, 11 . . .' A Co-op delivery van. The Co-op was on the corner at the other end. The driver would have just enough time to reach it before the barriers were put up there, too.

'4, 3, 2, 1,' Gran said. 'No, wait. Let this one through, he was already indicating. It's not worth getting run over just to prove a point. All right. Lift off!'

She went out into the middle of the road and held out her arms like a lollipop lady, while Ahmed and Abdul stood the uprights in a row, laid the crossbars on them and hung the signs. The sandbags, which were there to keep the uprights steady, lay at their feet like sleeping puppies. As they walked away one driver hooted crossly, but it was too late. They had closed the road.

Ahmed and Abdul took off at a run, but Connie helped Gran to park the barrow at No. 248, and they walked back together, looking at the notices on telephone poles that explained that the road would be closed for the Lancaster Street Party, reminding people to move their cars in time. Halfway down Brookes Road and Union Street were more barriers. In Brookes Road the big tent was already going up.

'People could move those barriers,' Connie said.

'They won't touch them now they're up,' Gran said. 'They're official. We got permission from the council. But they've got to be moveable. We have to let emergency vehicles through: ambulances, fire engines. If it was my house on fire we'd be glad enough to see them.'

Gran's house was nearer to the top end,

just past Union Street. People were setting up long tables borrowed from the community centre, and while Gran and Connie had been gone, someone else had brought out strings of flags to hang across the street. Mrs Hussain, Ahmed's and Abdul's mum, was leaning dangerously out of her upstairs window, tying one end of a string to the gutter above her head. Ahmed had climbed a street light and was fixing the other end of the string to the top of it.

A lady was laying out face-paints on a table in case anyone wanted to be turned into a tiger or a vampire. The girls from four doors down had painted the kerb stones red, yellow and green outside their house, and a man and a boy whom Connie did not know were chalking white lines across the road. Later on there would be games and races.

Connie did not really know anyone apart from Ahmed and Abdul, and she only knew them because their family was friends with Gran. She had never stayed with Gran on her own before. Usually she came with Mum and the three of them did things together, but Mum was working now, and Dad had driven her over by herself.

When she was with Mum she had noticed all the other children in the street, but now that she had a chance to look at them closely she saw that they were all older than she was, or very much smaller. Abdul said he was in year 4, the same as she was, but Abdul had friends of his own, all boys. When he wasn't with them he played kindly with his little sisters in the back garden. Connie could see them from her window. They had a shed at the end of the path and they walked up and down with carrier bags, wearing bits of curtain on their heads, playing at grown-up ladies going to the supermarket. Abdul stood in the shed and sold them snail shells and empty matchboxes.

They probably thought that Connie was too big to play with them. They were wrong.

2

The Boxing Club was a long, low building on the corner of Union Street. Connie had always been afraid of it when she was small, hearing the thumps and shouts echoing inside, behind closed doors and high windows, but one evening she and Mum and Gran had been walking past when the boxers came out. Connie had thought that they would go on hitting each other, right there in the street, but they were very quiet and polite, just unchained their bicycles and rode away into the dusk.

Today the doors were wide open and there was a notice pinned up: EXHIBITION. Connie looked in. The boxing ring, which was square, stood in the middle inside its ropes, and long leather punch-bags hung from the ceiling like giant aubergines, but there was no boxing going on. All around the walls were photographs, dozens of photographs, of Lancaster Street through the ages, and all the people who had lived in it, right up to now. Some of the photographs were brown and faded and most of them were quite small or cut out of newspapers with columns of tiny print. Gran was very interested but Connie knew she would get bored and thought it was safer to leave before she did.

'I don't *have* to go to the party, do I?' Connie said.

'I thought you were looking forward to it,' Gran said.

'I don't know anybody. They might not talk to me.'

'That's what the party's for,' Gran said.

'This is a long street. People who live at one end never meet the people at the other. Nearly everyone here goes out to work – a lot of the others are students. In winter you can go for weeks without even seeing the people who live opposite. It's dark when we go out and it's dark when we come home. This is a chance for us all to get together.'

'But can I come back to yours if I don't like it?'

'Of course you can. Just come and find me if you get fed up. I don't suppose anyone's going to be partying all day.'

Connie went out into the street, just to have a look. From the corner of Brookes Road she could hear music. That was the signal for the party to start. It was CDs for now; later on there would be a live band, which was why they were down at Brookes Road. A little way up from Gran's, on the

other side of the street, was Holdstock
Close, where there were sheltered flats for
old people who might not want to hear
dance music at midnight.

'Are you going to get a sheltered flat?'
Connie asked Gran.

'One day, maybe,' Gran said. 'But I don't
think I need sheltering just yet.'

There were already crowds gathering out
in the roadway; the zigzag strings of flags
were stirring in the breeze. Grown-ups
stood talking; children – she had not known
there were so many children – were coming
out of houses. Abdul ran up to her with his
three little sisters all holding hands, like a
string of flags themselves, bright and
fluttering.

'Can you look after them for a minute?'
Abdul said, and put the hand of the biggest
little sister into Connie's hand. Now she was
holding the string.

The little girls looked up at her and grinned and giggled.

'He won't come back,' the biggest one said. 'He wants to play cricket while there aren't any cars.'

Lancaster Street sloped down, then up again, with a flat stretch between the slopes. In the distance, beyond Brookes Road, Connie could see the cricket game, already in progress. The sisters giggled some more.

'What do *you* want to do?' Connie said. Sneaky Abdul. But she did not mind. Now she was not on her own.

'We want to run in the races,' they all said, as if they had rehearsed it. 'This way.'

The races were being run where the chalk marks were drawn on the road. A man was sorting out little children. When he saw Connie coming with her string of sisters, he looked pleased.

Road Closed

'We're doing the smallest ones first. Can you help line them up? Connie, isn't it?'

Connie stared. How did he know? She'd never seen him before. The man laughed.

'I know Janey – your gran. I'm Joe, and that's my wife, doing the face-painting.'

Connie helped Joe with the races and when it was time for the bigger ones to have a turn the race track grew longer, all the way down from Union Street to the edge of the cricket game.

The cricketers stopped and got out of the way. Some of them even joined in. When Connie lined up for her race she found Abdul beside her. Abdul was sure to win; he ran everywhere, all the time. Connie thought that if she just tried to keep up with Abdul he would certainly beat her but she would probably beat everyone else.

Her cunning plan worked. Abdul came first and she was second, and won a box of party poppers. All the prizes were things like that, to help the party go well. The little ones got helium balloons whether they won or not. Connie tied the balloons to their wrists, in case they got away.

The houses at either end of the finishing line were 173 on one side and 182 on the other. An old lady was looking over the gate of 182. Connie had noticed her earlier, clapping at the end of each race, no matter who won.

'Having fun?' the old lady said.

The sisters nodded and giggled. Connie thought that someone had better say something.

'Yes, thank you.'

'I thought I knew everyone in the street,' the old lady said. 'I know these three. Are you new?'

'I'm staying with my gran,' Connie said. 'Up the other end.'

Road Closed

'We lived at the other end when we were children,' the old lady said. 'There were lots of parties then but we were never allowed to go. We lived with my aunt and uncle in the big house. She thought street parties were common – so she said. If you ask me, she didn't believe in having fun. We used to watch through the window, just like we do now.'

She turned and pointed, and at the upstairs window Connie saw another old lady, looking down and waving.

Connie waved back. 'Why don't you come to this one? Everyone can.'

'We're a bit past it, now,' the old lady said. 'She's in bed and I'm on sticks. No, we have to get our fun watching other people enjoying themselves. So make sure you do enjoy yourselves – we're counting on you.'

The sisters were tugging at Connie's hand. She said goodbye and went to find

Gran. She felt she *had* to enjoy herself now,
for the sake of the two old ladies, or rather,
for the little girls they had once been.

3

Gran was putting out paper plates and napkins on the long tables. People were coming out of the houses with bowls and dishes, heaped with food.

'It's not so bad, then?' Gran said, when she saw Connie running towards her with the string of sisters. 'Want to help? If you go over to the Boxing Club you'll find jugs of juice. Your helpers can bring the plastic cups.'

'Do you know their names?' Connie said. 'When I ask they just giggle.'

'Sahir, Rahib and Rukhsana,' Gran said, 'but it doesn't matter. Whatever you say, they all answer at once.' Sahir, Rahib and Rukhsana burst out laughing. Gran smiled.

'Why worry? They love you already.'

The sisters went with Connie to fetch the drinks from the Boxing Club, they stayed with her during lunch, and for the rest of the afternoon, wherever she went, Sahir, Rahib and Rukhsana were behind her in a string, holding hands.

Sometimes other little children tagged along, but they always went away again. The sisters hung on. When they went to watch the cricket, Abdul saw them standing in a row and looked guilty.

'You want to leave them with me?' he said, but before she could answer they all let go of each other and clung to her. Rukhsana began to cry.

'No,' Connie said. 'I'll keep them.'

She wished that she really could keep them. She had always wanted a brother but now she thought that there couldn't be anything better than sisters who loved you.

She would have to speak to Mum when she got home.

There was another girl on the end of the string now. Someone in the big tent put on a bhangra CD and the girl let go of Rukhsana's hand and began to dance, all on her own in the middle of the street. The sisters immediately rushed out and joined her, stamping and swaying, still wearing their balloons, though Rukhsana had trouble staying upright even when she had both feet on the ground.

Someone said, 'I couldn't do that.'

Connie looked round. There were two more girls standing beside her. 'Do what?'

'Dance in the street like that.'

'Yes you can. We can do anything we like, today.'

'I'm going to, then,' the smaller girl said.

'You'll catch it if Auntie sees—'

'Don't care. Watch me!' She skipped out

into the road and danced and twirled with the sisters. Other people were joining in now.

'Look at me, Edie! Come on!'

'I'm staying here,' Edie said. 'You go on if you want,' she said to Connie. 'Don't let me stop you.'

She sounded cross, and because her hair was cut dead level with her eyebrows, she seemed to be scowling too. But Connie knew that she was really saying, 'Don't go. Stay and talk.'

'I don't like dancing either,' she said.

'Oh, I *like* it, all right,' Edie said. 'But I'll be for it if Joan gets dirty or tears her frock. She's always tearing something.'

Joan was wearing pink frills, not the sort of thing for a street party, more what people got done up in if their mothers wanted to show them off. Edie was wearing a frock too, not so frilly but with puffed sleeves. It

24

was white and silky, with net over the skirt. Connie hoisted herself on to a garden wall but Edie stayed standing. Connie could see why. The wall was mossy, the sort of green that would come off on pale clothes if you sat on it.

Joan dropped out of the dance and came over. 'Those girls have got balloons. Can I have a balloon, Edie? Can I?'

'Haven't got any money,' Edie growled.

'Oh, they didn't buy them,' Connie said. 'They won them in the races – well, they didn't really win them, everybody got one. Have one of these.'

There was a bunch of balloons fixed to the gate beside them.

'That'd be stealing,' Edie said.

'No, they're for all of us. No one'll mind.'

'Races?' Joan said. 'Can I go in a race?'

'They're all finished now,' Edie said. 'Didn't you see?'

Road Closed

Joan's mouth turned down. Her lip began to tremble. Even the big white bow in her hair seemed to droop.

'Cry-baby,' Edie said, but she did not look very happy herself.

'We'll have our own races,' Connie said quickly. 'Look, we can do it in Union Street, there's nothing going on there.'

She jumped down and untied the bunch of balloons from the gate.

'Come on, Joan, see how many you can win.'

'Don't you go falling over,' Edie said, but she was starting to smile.

4

As soon as Connie got off the wall, Sahir, Rahib and Rukhsana stopped dancing and rushed after her, balloons bobbing. It would be more fun for Joan if they were running as well, more like the real thing. No one could have too many balloons. Edie sat on the steps of the Boxing Club to watch, on a clean bit at the side where nobody walked.

Connie lined them all up by the ROAD CLOSED sign where the next street cut across.

Joan spelled out the letters. 'What's that for?'

'So the cars won't run us over.'

'Silly, there aren't any cars. Only the milkman's horse.'

Connie did not argue. Little children said the oddest things.

If Joan wanted to imagine the milkman galloping up the road, bottles clinking, instead of crawling along in his float, why spoil it for her? 'I'm going back to the Boxing Club,' she said. 'When I hold my hand up, you get ready, and when I say go, you run.'

Rukhsana fell over after three steps and finished her race on all fours. Rahib could only trot, but Sahir was kind and ran very slowly so that her sisters would always be in front.

Joan did not understand. 'What's the point of races if you don't try to win?'

'But you win every time,' Connie said, handing out balloons.

'You mean I should do it like her?' Joan pointed at Sahir.

'You run with us, next time,' Edie said, 'and you'll be last. See how you like that.

'She's used to being the baby,' she explained to Connie. 'Wait till she comes out of the kindergarten, she'll soon find out.'

'What's a kindergarten?'

'Baby school,' Edie said. 'Didn't you ever go to one?'

'We called it the infants,' Connie said. *'We're* going to race now,' she said to Sahir. 'You stand by the one-way sign and say Ready-steady-go!'

She lined up with Edie and Joan, but when Sahir said 'Go!' she and Edie ran very slowly and Joan won again.

'We're too soft, that's our trouble,' Edie sighed.

The Hussain sisters were sitting on the steps of the Boxing Club, giggling and pointing.

'What's the matter?' Connie said.

'You look funny running on your own,' Rahib said.

'Don't look any funnier than you,' Edie snapped. She muttered to Connie, 'Why are they all dressed up like that? Is it fancy dress?'

'It's what they always wear, shalwar-kameez. They're Muslims.'

'Muslims come from abroad.'

'No they don't, they're English.' Where do *you* come from? Connie thought. Never seen girls in shalwar-kameez? Don't you ever look out of the window? What about school?

Joan came up with the three balloons she had won.

'They haven't got faces on.'

'This kind don't.'

'Theirs have.' She looked at the sisters with their helium balloons.

'Oh, stop moaning,' Edie said. 'You won't be able to take them home anyway. Auntie won't have them in the house.'

Connie had a bright idea. 'Just a moment.' She ran across to Joe's wife at the face-painting table.

'Could you put a face on a balloon for me – for a little girl,' she added, in case anyone thought she wanted it for herself. 'Could you do a tiger?'

'I should have thought of that myself,' Mrs Joe said, laughing, and drew a fierce tiger face with green eyes on an orange balloon.

When she got back to the Boxing Club the Hussain sisters had started a game of their own, seeing how many steps they could jump down in one go. Connie tied the tiger balloon to Joan's wrist and she went off, beaming, to jump with the others. They took no notice of her, but now that she was enjoying herself she did not seem to mind.

'Don't you fall over and get dirty!' Edie called. 'You know what Auntie will say. I hope that stuff doesn't come off on her frock,' she fretted, looking at the tiger.

'Your auntie sounds a right old crab,' Connie said. 'Is she here?'

'Not her,' Edie said. 'And she'd have a fit if she knew we were. She doesn't hold with parties. But she's out visiting, we nipped through the back fence. I don't care,' she said, 'but it's rotten for Joan. She never has anyone to play with.'

'What about your mum?' Connie said.

'She's dead,' Edie said. 'So's Daddy. Everyone says we should be grateful to Auntie for taking us in, but I've heard her telling people it's her Christian duty. She doesn't really want us.'

Connie wished she had not asked. 'I expect she does really.'

'Uncle Wallace is all right,' Edie said, 'but he's away a lot. *She* won't let us play in the street, so we never make any friends.'

'Well, I didn't know anybody, hardly, this morning, and now I've got Sahir and Rahib and Rukhsana. And you've got all of us, haven't you?'

Edie smiled properly this time.

'You can come to my gran's to play, can't you?' Connie said. 'She lives at 35.'

'We're just over the road, then,' Edie said. 'The big house.'

'I know, I'll get her to ask your auntie – and we can play in the back garden with the Hussains.'

'Them?' Edie said, looking at Sahir and Rahib and Rukhsana leaping up and down the steps with Joan. She was still smiling. 'It'll be like having a whole lot of new sisters, all at once.'

'That's what I thought,' Connie said.

5

The sun went down at eight o'clock, exactly opposite the end of Lancaster Street, so that all the houses turned pink and shadows stretched for metres.

The CDs had been put away and the band was playing. Grown-ups were dancing now, which made Sahir and Rahib and Rukhsana fall about laughing. Edie looked disapproving.

'That's not proper dancing,' she said. 'Not like we do with Madame Smith.'

'Who's she?'

'My dancing teacher, of course. I'd like to do acrobatic and tap, but Auntie says it's vulgar. I don't know what Madame would call all that hopping about,' Edie said, but after a bit she laughed too.

Most of the children were still up, although some were beginning to look sleepy. All the way down the street people had brought out carpets and mats and laid them across the road. They were sitting on them to eat and the littlest children were falling asleep on cushions. Some of the balloons had got loose and they floated away into the sunset, except for the ones that snagged on trees and telephone wires. Those were the helium balloons. The ones with ordinary human breath in them drifted along the road, sometimes bouncing if a draught caught them. Joan still had her tiger.

As it grew dark, candles were lit and lanterns stood on garden walls. There was no wind now; the flames burned steadily as the darkness thickened. Gran's friend Joe was sitting on a carpet with his wife and children, and their children. Gran was dancing, which Connie thought was odd. She hadn't known that old people danced like that, but perhaps Gran wasn't so very old, not like the people in the sheltered flats at Holdstock Close. Certainly not as old as the lady at 182 who had spoken to Connie after the races.

'Come and have some food,' Joe said.

'All of us?'

'Of course, there's plenty.'

Connie and the Hussain sisters sat down on the carpet.

'Us too?' Joan said.

'He said all of us, didn't he?'

'Don't spoil your supper,' Edie warned, 'or Auntie'll want to know why. We've got guests tonight.'

Joe was passing round a plate of wraps with salad inside and they all took one, but as soon as the three sisters had sat down they became very quiet, and Rukhsana had curled up and fallen asleep with the wrap in her hand, before she had taken even a bite of it.

'She's only little,' Sahir said, but the next time Connie looked Sahir was asleep too, and Rahib. Edie and Joan had gone; she saw two small figures disappearing into the darkness, like moths, one white, one pink. The tiger balloon was lying among the cushions.

Gone to the loo, she thought, and decided she might as well go herself now that the sisters were asleep. She could nip back to Gran's without having to leave them all outside on the landing, giggling.

Gran had been home to put on the lights and turn on the radio – 'Just in case a burglar tries his luck.' Connie went into the front bedroom, opened the window and looked out.

All the way down to the main road the orange lights glowed on their lampposts and below them gleamed the little flames of the candles and lanterns. The band was playing loudly, far down the road, but under that sound was another, like a purring roar: dozens of people talking to each other.

On her left was Joe's carpet and beyond that another, an even bigger one, that stretched from one side of the road to the other, and then a long thin one that looked as if it had once been on a staircase. The people on that carpet sat in a row. Gran had put out an old hearth rug opposite the front gate in case anyone needed a spare, but no one was using it.

Then she noticed another carpet, on the right. She had thought that Gran's rug was the last, but it was quite dark just there, on the corner of Holdstock Close, where the street light was not working properly. It just flickered dully every now and again, and went out. She could see people sitting there, but not who they were. And the people were not sitting on the carpet, they had armchairs and a settee, and a low table with a vase of flowers on it, just as if they were sitting at home in their own living room, watching telly.

6

Connie leaned out further, trying to see if they did have a television set. She was sure that the carpet had not been there earlier, and although she had been rushing about all day she was sure that she would have noticed people shifting furniture. But then, the carpet was not in the middle of Lancaster Street, like all the others, it was in the turning to Holdstock Close. Perhaps the people were afraid that one of those emergency vehicles would come roaring up the road and drive over their carpet, but in Holdstock Close they would not be in anyone's way. That was why they had brought out the big chairs and the settee.

Somebody got up off the settee, crossed

the carpet and switched on the light. It was a proper light, a tall standard lamp with a big shade. That was really odd. Fancy bringing out an electric light as well. Why didn't they use candles like everyone else, or one of those lanterns that were standing on garden walls all down the street?

The carpet was in its own little patch of light now, like a moonlit island in a dark sea. Out of the darkness came a woman pushing a trolley with cakes and sandwiches on it. Behind her came Edie, carrying a tray with cups and saucers, and behind Edie was Joan, walking very carefully, with a teapot. The teapot was wearing a woolly hat with a pompom on top, the handle sticking out at one side and the spout at the other.

They might have invited *me*, Connie thought, remembering how Edie and Joan had sat with the Hussains and Joe's family, although she didn't remember seeing them eat anything. But of course, Edie had told Joan, 'Don't spoil your supper', and there, on the bottom shelf of the trolley, was a big iced cake with a frill.

They wouldn't mind if I went down, though, Connie told herself. If I just went and said hello. She was full of food, she did not actually want any cake, she just wanted to be offered a piece, the way she would be on anyone else's carpet.

Now Edie and Joan were handing round sandwiches to the grown-ups who sat in the armchairs and on the settee. Connie was certain that she could smell food cooking too. Perhaps Edie's auntie had put something in the oven for later, after the tea and cake . . . but it wasn't exactly the smell of cooking, more the smell of burning, smoke, but there was nothing on fire –

There was something on fire somewhere.

In the distance she could hear a siren whooping, coming closer, but still a long way off, on the main road.

Then something caught her eye, a flash, a blue flash. She looked away from Edie and her family on their carpet and craned her neck to see down to the other end of the street. There, at the junction, where the blue flashes were coming from, a vehicle had stopped at the corner: a fire engine. It was going to come up Lancaster Street. The firefighters must be moving the barriers.

All down the street people had realized what was happening. They were getting up, running to the pavements, grabbing beanbags and cushions and children. Mrs Hussain and Ahmed were carrying off the sisters. Others were shifting the long tables and already the headlamps were boring up the street, with the flashing blue lights above them and the siren hee-hawing.

The people on Edie's carpet took no notice at all. Edie's auntie was pouring tea now and Joan was kneeling by the trolley, looking at the cake. Well, they didn't have to worry, they were out of the way there, at the entrance to Holdstock Close, but surely they'd heard the racket? Wouldn't they even look?

Gran was at the gate calling, 'Connie! *Connie!*'

'I'm up here,' Connie called.

'Oh, thank heavens for that. You stay there,' Gran said; at least, that was what Connie thought she said, for the fire engine was almost level with them now, driving over the carpets, siren blaring. It was impossible to hear any other sound. Even the band was drowned out.

Then the fire engine passed Gran's house and slowed down. Where was the fire?

It turned left.

It drove into Holdstock Close.

It drove straight over the carpet and through the furniture: the settee and the armchairs, the tea trolley and the standard lamp, and through the grown-ups, and Joan, and Edie.

7

Connie was too shocked even to cry out. She turned from the window, threw herself down on the big bed with her face in the pillow so that she could not see, and her fingers in her ears so that she could not hear.

Even so, she could not blot out the siren until it stopped on its own. Slowly she took her fingers out of her ears, the left, then the right. There were no shrieks or screams, no moans, only voices and footsteps down in the street, and the band in the distance, and other footsteps coming up the stairs in a hurry. She looked round.

The light on the landing showed her someone standing in the doorway. It was Gran. Connie started to cry.

'Are they all dead?'

Gran sat down on the bed and put her arms around her.

'No one's dead, darling. There's not even any flames.'

'Not the fire. Not the *fire*. Edie and Joan – run over—'

'Shh, shh, nothing like that. If the fire was that bad we'd have noticed. It's probably a smoke alarm gone off at the sheltered flats. Joe's gone to find out.'

'But the fire engine – it went right over them.'

'No one's been hurt,' Gran said. 'We all saw the engine coming. We could hardly miss it, could we? Everyone got out of the way.'

Partly, Connie wanted to go and look, out of the window, but even more she wanted to stay safely on the bed with Gran's arms around her.

'Edie didn't. Edie and Joan and her auntie and uncle—'

'*Who?*'

'They were having tea on the carpet.'

'Everybody got off their carpets,' Gran said. 'As soon as we saw the flashing blue lights we cleared everything out of the road, even before they'd got the barriers down. There may be a few squashed samosas lying about and the carpets will never be the same again, but they weren't up to much to start with. I've been looking for an excuse to get rid of my dreadful old rug for ages.'

How could she be so calm? How could she make jokes?

'But *they* didn't get out of the way. They didn't move anything. They had big chairs and a settee and a lamp and a tea trolley like yours, only it was wooden.'

'Are you sure you weren't asleep at that window?' Gran said. She got up, crossed the room and peered out. 'Darling, I promise you, there's nothing down there but carpets, no settees or tea trolleys – and certainly no corpses. Connie, you *must* have been dreaming, or imagining it. Come and look.'

Connie got up, very slowly, and went to stand beside Gran. Between No. 28 and No. 26 was the mouth of Holdstock Close. From walls and windows she could see the reflections of the blue lights, still flashing, somewhere in the close. Then she made herself look down at the roadway to where Edie and her family had been having tea, serving sandwiches, and Joan had been picking a bit of loose icing off the cake, where she sat by the tea trolley, under the standard lamp, on the carpet, the red carpet with a pattern that ran right round the edge.

There was no carpet. There was nothing in the road at all except double yellow lines on both sides, to stop people parking by the corner.

'Now do you believe me?' Gran said. 'What did you think you saw?'

'They were having tea,' Connie said, 'like they were in the front room. They had sandwiches and a cake. And a teapot with a bobble hat.'

'Who were?'

'Edie and Joan.'

'Darling, who are Edie and Joan?'

'They were at the party,' Connie said. 'They were with us all day.'

'With who? You and Sahir and Rahib and Rukhsana? I didn't see anyone with you.'

'You were dancing.'

'Yes, but I saw you.'

'They were with me when I had supper on Joe's carpet. And then the little ones went to sleep. They must have gone home to their auntie.'

'I don't know an Edie and Joan,' Gran said. 'Perhaps they're just visiting, like you.'

'She said – Edie said – they lived up here, just across the road. And the fire engine went right over them.'

'Connie, believe me, nothing went over anybody. Come down now and see.'

8

They went downstairs, out into the street. The band was still playing. Out of the way, in Brookes Road, it had gone on playing even while the fire engine went by. There on the tarmac, on the left, was Joe's carpet, and the long runner where people had sat in a line like a queue, then Gran's rug opposite the gate. And there was the dark gap where the street light had broken, leading to Holdstock Close. And there were the double yellow lines, and nothing else; no carpet, no lamp, no furniture, no cake, no Edie, no Joan.

Down in Holdstock Close the fire engine was still flashing and out of the darkness Joe came walking.

'Everything all right?' Gran said.

'Yes, but they were only just in time. If that smoke alarm hadn't gone off when it did there'd have been a real blaze. Someone left an electric ring on under a saucepan, in the flats. Hello, Connie, whatever's the matter?'

'Bad dream,' Gran said. 'She thought she saw something.'

'I did see–'

'Of course you did, but it wasn't what you thought you saw, was it? It couldn't have been.'

'It was people having tea on a carpet,' Connie said to Joe. 'And the fire engine went right over them.' Perhaps he would believe her.

Gran said something very quietly to Joe. She thought that Connie could not hear. 'You've lived here longer than I have,' she said. 'Was there ever a house standing there, before they built the close?'

'There may have been,' Joe said. 'Now's the time to find out,' he added. 'Down at the Boxing Club,'

'The photographs!' Gran said. 'We can go and look tomorrow.'

'Look at what?' Connie said.

'In the morning. I think it's time you went to bed.'

'Is it about what I saw? I want to know now.'

While they were talking they had been walking back to Gran's house. Under the porch light Connie saw Joe and Gran look at each other.

'What *is* it?' Connie wailed. 'Did I see ghosts?'

'Oh dear,' Joe said. 'You think you saw ghosts having tea?'

'It wasn't just tea,' Gran said. 'She thinks she was with them all day.'

'Scary ghosts, were they?' Joe said.

'Hollow eyes, rattling bones, green teeth?'

'Stop it!' Gran said, but Connie knew what he meant.

'No, they were ordinary, like me. I didn't know they were ghosts.'

'Then they probably were,' Joe said, as if it were the most normal thing in the world. 'Ghosts are only people, after all. You don't know they're ghosts until they walk through the wall.'

'They didn't walk through the wall,' Connie said. 'They were real.'

But now she began to remember. Gran hadn't seen them and nor had the sisters. That was what Rahib must have meant after the races. 'You look funny running on your own.'

'They were on your carpet. Joan left her balloon behind.'

'The one with the tiger face?' Joe said. 'I thought it was yours.'

'Didn't *you* see them either?'

'I wasn't really looking,' Joe said, carefully. 'And it was dark. Are you going to be awake all night, worrying, if you don't find out, right this minute?'

Connie nodded.

'Fair enough,' said Gran. 'Let's go and look. The Club's still open.'

Now that the fire was out and no one had to worry, people had gone back to their carpets, the band was playing and people were dancing again.

Connie and Gran and Joe and Joe's wife walked down to the Boxing Club and went in. It was empty now; they had the place to themselves.

'We'll start at the door and go all the way round so we don't miss anything,' Gran said.

Connie wondered why she had thought that the photographs would be dull. True, a lot of them were brown and blurry and she did not know the people in them, but now she had something to look for, although she could not imagine how she would feel if she saw Edie and Joan looking back at her from some picture taken long ago.

9

The pictures nearest to the door were the oldest, Lancaster Street in the 1870s when it was just a farm track with three cottages and a barn. As they went along the row more houses were built, the muddy lane became a proper road with street lights, there was a pavement on the right-hand side, then on the left.

Then there were people, women in strange long bulky skirts and big hats, men with beards and moustaches, and there were children. There was a street party in 1897 for Queen Victoria's Diamond Jubilee, another in 1902 for the Coronation of Edward VII, another for the Coronation of George V, then George VI, and last of all for Queen Elizabeth II in 1953. Year after year long tables stood in the road, strings of flags hung above them, just like now.

All the time, behind the children and the flags and the tables, the street was changing. More and more houses went up, but it was difficult to tell which part of the street they were looking at unless they spotted a familiar building.

'That's the Bricklayer's Arms,' Mrs Joe said, 'before they built the extension.'

'There's the Boxing Club.'

'Here, this is our end,' Joe said suddenly. 'George V, Silver Jubilee Party, 1935. Look, there's the Co-op on the corner. Mind you, I don't suppose it was a Co-op then.'

Connie stared at the photograph. There was the three-storey house, No. 30, opposite Gran's, and No. 28 beside it, and then a long house with three chimney stacks next to that, exactly where Holdstock Close was now. And yet, there was something about that house . . .

Gran and Joe were peering at it too.

'That's number 26,' Gran said. 'But look, it's twice the size it is now.'

'That must have been where the fire was,' Joe said.

'It *is* where the fire was,' Connie said. 'Where the engine turned left.'

'I didn't mean tonight's fire,' Joe said, 'not in Holdstock Close. There was a fire in this street back in the 1950s, the Wallaces' place. Edith told me once that they used to live up this end.'

'Was it a bad fire?' Connie said. 'Did they die?'

'I don't think anyone died,' Mrs Joe said. 'The Miss Wallaces didn't. They live down at 182 now.'

'No smoke alarms in those days,' Gran said. 'So half the house must have gone and where it used to stand they cut through and built Holdstock Close.'

'Well,' Joe said, 'it looks as though you saw the ghost of a house. You even saw the ghost of a teapot.'

'But what about the people?'

'What were they called again, your friends?' Gran said. 'Didn't you say Edie?'

'Edie and Joan.'

'But that *is* the Miss Wallaces,' Mrs Joe said. 'Edith and Joan. Well, you can stop worrying about that, Connie. They're both alive.'

'Not only that,' Joe said, 'you were talking to Edith earlier today, after the race. She came to the gate, remember?'

'That wasn't Edie. She was old, ever so old.'

'She'd be about 80, I suppose,' Mrs Joe said, 'and Joan must be pushing 75. They're neither of them very strong, Connie, but they're not dead.'

'They aren't Edie and Joan,' Connie said. 'They can't be. They were children.'

'To tell you the truth,' Gran said, 'I'm not sure who you saw or what, but we seem to have a happy ending. No one died in that fire and no one died in the fire tonight, and no one got run over by a fire engine. I think it's safe for you to go to bed.'

Next morning Connie went with Gran and Abdul and Ahmed to help take down the barriers. Sahir, Rahib and Rukhsana wanted to come and watch, but Lancaster Street was not safe now that the barriers were coming down. They had to stay behind their front gate and wave. Connie promised to come and play supermarkets later. She would never be playing with Edie, now.

Joe and some friends were collapsing the big tent in Brookes Road; tables were being folded up. The flags were being lowered

Road Closed

but a few balloons were still drifting from wires and twigs. Connie saw the orange tiger caught in a hedge and rescued it. The chalk marks were still in the road and the carpets lay where they had been left last night – except for the one in Holdstock Close.

At 182 the old lady was in the front garden and her sister was looking through the window.

'Hello, Connie,' the old lady said. 'Did you enjoy the party?'

'Yes, thank you,' Connie said; then she remembered what they had been talking about last time. 'I'm sorry you couldn't come.'

Old Miss Wallace nodded to Gran. 'Is this your granddaughter? We were chatting yesterday. It's the oddest thing, I was telling her only then, that we were never allowed to go to street parties when we were children. But I've been thinking, and so's Joan. We're pretty sure we did go to one party, just the once. She says we ran races and won balloons, and danced in the street. I can't remember when it was, but I do know we had a wonderful time.'

There was a sharp rapping noise. At the upstairs window the other old lady was tapping on the glass and pointing, and smiling. Connie knew what she had seen.

She held out the tiger balloon to Miss Edith Wallace.

'Could you give this to Joan, please? I think it's hers.'

**Nelly the Monster Sitter:
Grerks, Squurms and Water Greeps**

Kes Gray

When Petronella Morton puts an ad in the local newspaper saying '**MONSTER SITTING AFTER SCHOOL AND WEEKENDS. CALL NELLY.**' little does she know that her phone will begin to ring. **AND RING AND RING AND RING.**

Nelly soon discovers that there are families of monsters living secretly all over the Montelimar Estate. Join her at three addresses for three monstrously different baby sitting adventures.

Funny, exciting and irreverent 'Nelly the Monster Sitter' stories will have huge appeal for boys and girls of 8 and above.

Also available:

**Nelly the Monster Sitter: Cowcumbers, Pipplewaks & Altigators
Nelly the Monster Sitter: Huffaluks, Muggots and Thermitts**

The Magician's Boy

Susan Cooper

Once upon a time there was a Boy who worked for a Magician.

He polished the Magician's wands and caught the rabbits that the Magician pulled out of hats. But what he wanted most of all was to learn magic himself.

Follow the Boy as he is transported to the Land of Story on a magical quest. Adventure and familiar characters are at every turn and a perfect ending awaits . . .

'Perfect for reading aloud, the tale will encourage readers and listeners to revisit familiar fairy tales and nursery rhymes' KIRKUS REVIEWS